ADA TWIST, SCIENTIST
Show Me the Bunny

By Gabrielle Meyer

Abrams Books for Young Readers • New York

It's Easter morning! Ada and Rosie are decorating eggs for the Twist Easter Egg Hunt, which is Ada's favorite family tradition.

Iggy presents his Easter masterpiece, the Leaning Tower of Egg-za!

Ada and Rosie are impressed. Iggy always comes up with the most amazing designs!

Mom and Dad come into the kitchen because they have a very important Easter announcement.
    This year's official egg hider will be . . . Ada!

Ada is thrilled! She's never been the official egg hider before.

"I'll make sure this is the best Twist Easter Egg Hunt ever," she promises. "Nothing will ruin it!"

At the sound of a loud *meowww*, everyone turns. "Mooshu, no!" cries Ada. But it's too late! Mooshu leaps and smashes into the tower. Eggs go flying all over the room!

Everyone runs and jumps and slides to catch the eggs! Arthur walks in right on time to catch the last egg before it goes SPLAT on the ground.

Phew! That was almost an Easter disaster!

Mom hands Arthur a basket for his eggs, but he says he doesn't need one. He's not doing the egg hunt this year.

"WHAT!?" gasps Ada. "You have to do the Easter egg hunt. It's a Twist family tradition!"

"It's always too easy for me to find the eggs," Arthur says. "It's not fun anymore."

As the official egg hider, Ada can't let her brother quit the egg hunt. Luckily, she has an idea.

"Let me hide some test eggs to show you how hard it will be," Ada proposes.

"Fine," agrees Arthur. "But if they're too easy to find, I'm not doing the egg hunt."

Ada, Iggy, and Rosie go to the backyard and brainstorm about how to hide eggs so they'll be super hard to find.

Iggy suggests building a shrink ray to make the eggs teeny-tiny. But the shrink ray might make them teeny-tiny, too, and they don't want to be bug-sized.

When Rosie tries to brainstorm, she gets distracted by something moving near the bushes. It looks like a bunny!

"Easter Bunny!" she shouts.

"Hmm, you might be onto something," says Ada. "The Easter Bunny is really good at hiding eggs."

"No," says Rosie. "That's not what I meant. I saw the Easter Bunny in the backyard. Look!"

Rosie points to the bushes, but Ada and Iggy don't see anything.

Rosie is confused. She's positive she just saw a bunny. Where'd it go?

Since they still don't see a bunny, they go back to brainstorming. Ada decides they should use their favorite hide-and-seek tricks to hide the eggs. Ada likes hiding in dark places, so she hides her egg in the shed.

Iggy likes hiding in surprising places, so he hides his egg in a flowerpot.

And Rosie likes hiding in places that are high up, so she'll hide her egg somewhere hard to reach. But as she looks for a hiding spot, she thinks she sees the bunny again. She gets so distracted that she forgets to hide her egg.

Oopsies! She quickly stuffs it in her pocket as Arthur comes outside.

Arthur spots the eggs right away. "One in the shed, one in the flowerpot, and one in Rosie's pocket. Guess I'm not doing the Easter egg hunt this year after all."

Ada begs Arthur to give them one more chance.

"Okay," says Arthur. "You can hide one more egg. But if I find it fast, I'm retiring from the egg hunt FOREVER."

Ada realizes she knows the perfect hiding place for an egg: Arthur's helicopter! They put an egg in the toy helicopter and fly it high up in the air. Arthur will never find this hiding spot!

But Arthur finds the hiding spot immediately. "Easy," he says, pointing to the sky. "The egg is in my helicopter."

Ada is devastated. "It's my first year as the official egg hider and I can't even hide eggs good enough for Arthur," she says. "I should just give up."

Iggy and Rosie tell Ada she can't give up. "If the Easter Bunny can hide eggs, so can we," says Rosie.

"Um, Rosie, what are you pointing at?" Iggy asks. "There's no bunny in the backyard."

"Yes, there is!" Rosie says. "She's right there. Just look a little closer." Ada and Iggy look closer. "Oh, wait! I do see a bunny!" says Ada.

"Me, too!" says Iggy. "But why didn't we see it before?"

Ada knows why. The bunny was camouflaged! That's when an animal blends into its surroundings for protection, like how a chameleon can change colors to match its background.

The color of the bunny's fur helped it blend into the backyard!

Ada and Iggy tell Rosie they're sorry for not believing her about the bunny.

"It's okay," says Rosie. "Camouflage makes things pretty hard to see."

This gives Ada an idea. "That's it! That's how we'll hide the eggs. By *camouflaging* them."

The three little scientists go to the lab to camouflage the eggs. "Since we're hiding them in the backyard, we've got to make them super dirty," explains Ada.

They cover the eggs in dirt, sticks, and leaves.

They hide a camouflaged egg in the backyard. It's so hard to see!

The Twist Easter Egg Hunt begins, and nobody can find any eggs. "This is the hardest Easter egg hunt I've ever done," Dad says.

"Hard, huh?" asks Arthur. "I'll be the judge of that." He joins the search, but he can't find any eggs either!

After a lot of searching, Arthur finally spots something in the bushes behind Ada.

"Thanks," says Rosie. "We got the idea from the Easter Bunny."
She points to the bunny in the bushes.

Arthur looks around, confused. "Huh? I don't see any bunny."

"*Egg*-zactly!" says Ada with a giggle. "Because it's camouflaged!"

Arthur is impressed. "You're a great egg hider, Lil A!" he exclaims. "You made me love the egg hunt again."

Ada hugs her brother. "Good," she says, "because the best part of the Twist Easter Egg Hunt is doing it with you."

Library of Congress Control Number 2021948106

ISBN 978-1-4197-6079-2

ADA TWIST ™/© Netflix. Used with permission.
Ada Twist, Scientist and the Questioneers created by Andrea Beaty and David Roberts
Book design by Brenda E. Angelilli

Printed and bound in U.S.A.
10 9 8 7 6 5 4 3 2 1

Abrams Books for Young Readers are available at special discounts when purchased in quantity for premiums and promotions as well as fundraising or educational use. Special editions can also be created to specification. For details, contact specialsales@abramsbooks.com or the address below.

ABRAMS The Art of Books
195 Broadway, New York, NY 10007
abramsbooks.com

Now it's your turn! Camouflage and hide these eggs to create your own Easter Egg Hunt.

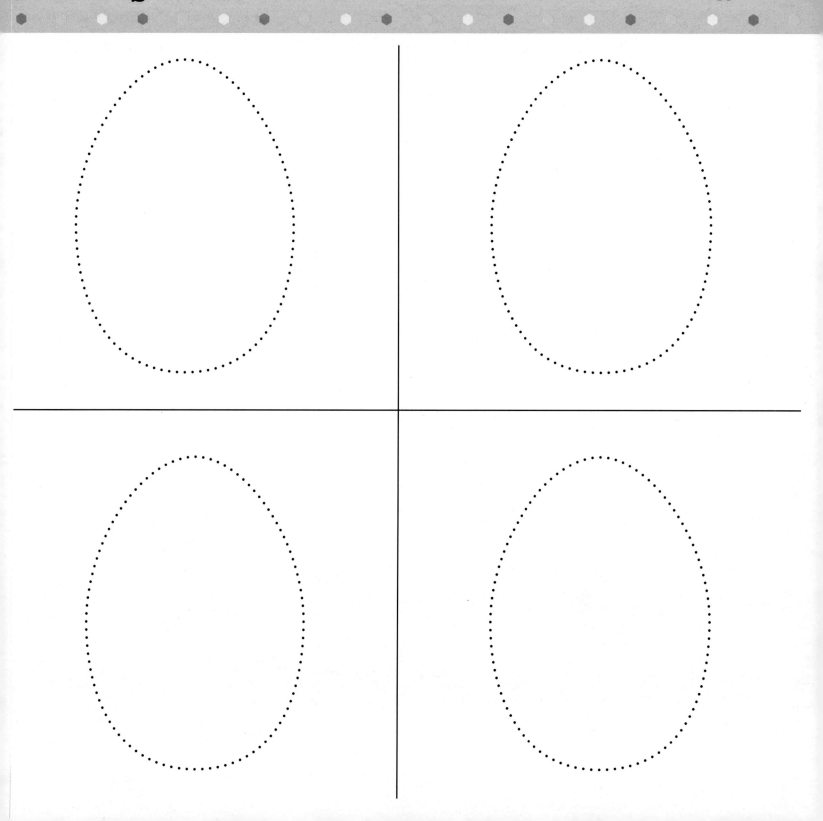